# Flint Saves the Day

by Michael Teitelbaum

illustrated by Carey Yost and Pete Oswald

Ready-to-Read

Simon Spotlight

New York   London   Toronto   Sydney

SIMON SPOTLIGHT
An imprint of Simon & Schuster
Children's Publishing Division
1230 Avenue of the Americas
New York, New York 10020

For information about special discounts for bulk purchases, please
contact Simon & Schuster Special Sales at 1-866-506-1949 or
business@simonandschuster.com.

Manufactured in the United States of America
First Edition 10 9 8 7 6 5 4 3 2 1
ISBN 978-1-4169-6497-1

Read the original book by
Judi Barrett and Ron Barrett.

My name is Flint Lockwood.
I live in Swallow Falls and
I am an inventor.
But I have to admit, not all of
my inventions turned out the way
I planned!

With my Spray-On Shoes, no one
would have to worry about
untied shoelaces ever again!
But I had not found a way
to get the shoes off!

My Ratbirds were cute—until
they started scaring people.

I also came up with something that let me know what Steve, my pet monkey, was thinking. But Steve got too excited!
At least he still likes me.

Then I came up with my greatest invention ever. It was a machine that I hoped would turn water into food. You see, Swallow Falls had a problem.
All anybody got to eat for breakfast, lunch, and dinner was sardines. Everyone was sick of sardines.

If my machine worked, Earl the
police officer would not
have to force his son, Cal,
to eat sardines.

The mayor could have
a tastier lunch.

And Brent could put
something else
in his sandwich.

I needed a lot of electric power
to make my machine work.
So I grabbed a power cable and
climbed up a tall electrical tower.
When this machine works, the people
of Swallow Falls will like me, I thought.

But when I plugged my machine in,
it suddenly zoomed off like a rocket
ship!
Then my invention shot into the sky
and was gone, just like that.

I felt terrible. My machine was a failure. I was a failure—again. Just then a news reporter named Sam Sparks came over with her cameraman, Manny.

"What's the matter?" she asked.

"My machine failed," I moaned.

"It was supposed to make any kind of food. Now people will have to keep eating sardines forever!"

A moment later something fell from
the sky. I picked it up.
"It's a piece of cheese," I said.
Then another piece fell.
"Cheese falling from the sky?" I asked.
"That can mean only one
thing. My machine is working!"

After that, cheeseburgers began
falling from the sky.
"It's raining cheeseburgers!" I cried.
"Your machine must be turning all
the water in the clouds into food!"
Sam explained.

All the people got very excited.
They gobbled up the cheeseburgers.
Then more food began raining down:
fried eggs, pancakes, and even pizza!
"This is great!" I shouted.

Everyone was happy to catch the falling food.

Word quickly spread about my machine.
Soon everyone wanted me to make
their favorite foods.
"May I please have waffles?" asked
one kid.
"Sure thing!" I said.

I typed "waffles" into my computer,
which sent a signal up to my
food-making machine.
"Falafel!" said Joe Towne.
"Jelly beans!" someone else said.
"Coming right up!" I said.

Even the mayor of Swallow Falls
asked for something. "Flint, my
boy," he said. "Can you do lunch?"
"Yes, I can!" I replied.
I typed in "sandwiches," and soon
they fell from the sky.

Police Officer Earl had a request too.
"Tomorrow is Cal's birthday,"
he said. "Can you make it rain
something special for him?"
"Of course," I said.

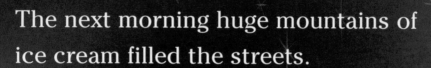

The next morning huge mountains of
ice cream filled the streets.
"So many flavors!" Cal said. "This
is awesome!"
Cal and his friends dove into the
ice cream.
Then I got hit with an ice cream
snowball!

I threw a snowball back.
"Snowball fight!" I shouted.

I saved the best treat for my
new friend, Sam. I built her
a huge castle made of Jell-O!
"Jell-O's my favorite," she said.
"I made this just for you," I said.
"Come on in."

We squished into the castle and
started jumping on the jiggly Jell-O.
We bounced high into the air.
"Thanks, Flint," Sam said. "This is
so great!"

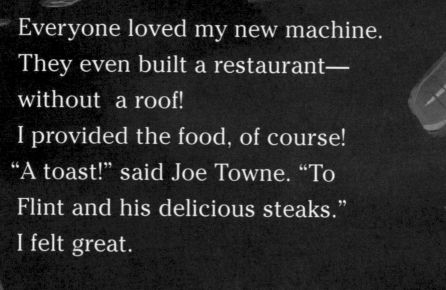

Everyone loved my new machine.
They even built a restaurant—
without  a roof!
I provided the food, of course!
"A toast!" said Joe Towne. "To
Flint and his delicious steaks."
I felt great.

Suddenly everything went wrong!
The food created by my machine
got bigger and bigger.
Giant food crashed down onto
houses and cars.

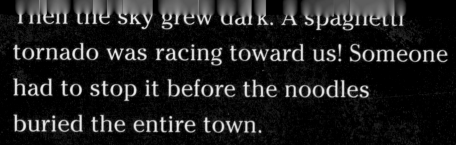

Then the sky grew dark. A spaghetti tornado was racing toward us! Someone had to stop it before the noodles buried the entire town.

"This is all my fault," I told Sam. "And I am the only one who can fix it."

I raced home to get my other
invention, a Flying Car.
"It will get us up to the machine,"
I said. "This is our only hope."
Sam, Steve, Brent, Manny, and I
took off. I steered around meatballs,
gummi bears, and pizza.

After a bumpy ride we finally
reached the machine.
"What now?" asked Sam.
"Take the controls, Manny," I said.
"I think I have a plan."

I had to stop my machine. And
I thought I knew how. I pulled out
a can of Spray-On Shoes, and sprayed
right into the food-making machine.
But before I could get back
to the Flying Car . . .

# KA-BOOM!

There was a huge explosion.
Sam, Manny, Steve, and Brent
had to return home without me.

Luckily a flock of Ratbirds
carried me safely to Earth.
"You did it!" Sam cried.
I smiled. This was the best day
of my life.